W9-AZD-542

animals**animals**

Anteaters

by **Renee C. Rebman**

mc **Marshall Cavendish**
Benchmark
New York

For my niece, Laura Ann Zajack

Series consultant:
James C. Doherty
General Curator, Bronx Zoo, New York

Marshall Cavendish Benchmark
99 White Plains Road
Tarrytown, New York 10591-9001
www.marshallcavendish.us

Library of Congress Cataloging-in-Publication Data
Rebman, Renée C., 1961-
Anteaters / by Renee Rebman.
p. cm.—(Animals, animals)
Summary: "Describes the physical characteristics, behavior, habitat, and endangered status of anteaters"—
Provided by publisher.
Includes bibliographical references and index.
ISBN-13: 978-0-7614-2234-1
ISBN-10: 0-7614-2234-X
1. Myrmecophagidae—Juvenile literature. I. Title. II. Series.
QL737.E24R43 2006
599.3'14—dc22
2005025611

Photo research by Joan Meisel

Cover Photo: Roland Seitre/Peter Arnold, Inc.

The photographs in this book are used by permission and through the courtesy of: *Alamy:* 7, Kevin Schafer; 16, 31, Danita Delimont; 39, Ricardo Beliel/Brazil Photos; *Animals Animals:* 1, Francois Savigny; 6, Fabio Medeiros Colombini; 9, Ruth Cole; 10, Martin Bruce; 15, Erwin & Peggy Bauer; 17, Richard La Val; 22, Fred Whitehead; 27, 33, Mark Jones; 36, Francois Savigny; 43, John Chellman; *Corbis:* 12, Michael & Patricia Fogden; 28, Joel Creed, Ecoscene; *Peter Arnold, Inc.:* 14, Gunter Ziesler; 25, Luiz C. Marigo; 32, Heinz Plenge; 34, Michael Sewell; 40, David Woodfall; *Photo Researchers, Inc.:* 4, Gerald C. Kelley; 37, Wesley Bocxe.

Editor: Mary Rich
Editorial Director: Michelle Bisson
Art Director: Anahid Hamparian
Series Designer: Adam Mietlowski

Printed in Malaysia

3 5 6 4 2

Contents

1 Introducing Anteaters

A giant anteater walks slowly across the sun-baked earth of a South American *savanna*. It sways back and forth awkwardly as it pushes its long snout along the ground. The tall grasses brush against the coarse gray and brown hair that covers its body. White diagonal stripes cut across its back, helping it to blend in with its surroundings. *Predators* that may want to eat it have difficulty seeing it. The anteater can search for food without being noticed.

It stops and sniffs the ground and begins tapping the dry earth with its long, curved claws. Its sensitive nose detects the delicious aroma of ants. The anteater begins to dig. Once it reaches the underground nest

The giant anteater walks on its knuckles, curving its long claws inward.

its long tongue will sweep up hundreds of ants. The anteater will spend most of the day eating crunchy ants and termites. It must eat thousands of the small, wriggling insects to satisfy its enormous appetite.

Anteaters are odd-looking creatures. Their bodies developed over many, many centuries to adapt to

Did You Know . . .
Although giant anteaters usually lumber along the ground, they can climb fairly well if they have to. In captivity, these animals have been observed climbing out of enclosures. Zookeepers have reported that the animals are quite limber. This climbing activity is not often seen in the wild.

The tail of a giant anteater is nearly as long as its body.

their surroundings. Their tubelike snouts and long, sticky tongues help them catch insects to eat. Their bushy tails help balance their bodies. Their long claws can be used for protection, as well as to dig. Anteaters may look clumsy, but they are very strong survivors.

A baby anteater rides on its mother's back. The baby is camouflaged from enemies by its stripes.

7

Ancestors of the anteater first appeared on Earth about 65 million years ago. It is believed that anteaters once lived in North America. A land bridge existed that connected North and South America. The animals traveled south and began making a new life in the warmer climate of South America. Gradually, landforms shifted and were flooded over, and the animals were trapped in their new home.

Anteaters can be found from Argentina to parts of southern Mexico. Some anteaters live in the rain forests and others make their homes in wet, swampy areas. Giant anteaters have adapted to hot, dry climates, which is why they can be found rustling through the long grasses of the savannas. The savannas are large, open areas found outside of the great Amazon rain forest in Central and South America. For only a few months of the year, the savannas get heavy rain, which floods the land. Giant anteaters that live in the savannas can swim and are well equipped to survive these torrential rains.

Scientists classify all animal species in specific orders. Anteaters belong to a scientific order called Xenarthra. This order also includes other unusual animals: sloths and armadillos. The name for this

Armadillos belong to the same scientific order as anteaters. They are both xenarthrans.

Sloths, also xenarthrans, often hang from trees just like tamandua and pygmy anteaters.

order comes from the Greek language and describes the animals well. "Xeno" is the Greek word for "strange" and "anthron" is the Greek word for "joint." Anteaters, sloths, and armadillos look very different, but these animals all have two things in common. The first characteristic they share is also found in birds: their *pelvic* bones are fused together in a solid *girdle* of bone. The second characteristic is not found in any other animals. Xenarthrans' spines are unique. Between each *vertebra* they have three pairs of joints. Other animals have only one joint connecting each vertebra.

Anteaters are very *territorial*. They are solitary hunters and prefer to live alone. A single giant anteater usually lives in a large area of land about 1.5 miles (2.4 kilometers) square. Other anteaters stay in their own territories. If two anteaters happen to meet, they usually ignore each other and go their separate ways. They are quiet, gentle creatures, but their lives are quite interesting.

From Pygmys to Giants

There are actually three distinct types of anteaters. The smallest is about the size of a squirrel, and the largest can weigh more than 80 pounds (36.3 kilograms). The giant anteater is the most well known and strangest looking of the three, but its two smaller relatives are also fascinating.

The silky, or "pygmy," anteater is the smallest. It has soft, silky fur and is about 20 inches (50 centimeters) long. This little creature only weighs about 17 ounces (.48 kilograms). Pygmys are *nocturnal*, which means they are only active at night.

The pygmy anteater is also *arboreal*, meaning it lives its life high in the trees of the tropical forests. Its

A pygmy anteater can use its tail to grasp a tree limb.

paws have large grooved pads that enable the anteater to grip branches and hang on tight. The pygmy has a *prehensile* tail. The muscles of its tail are strong, and the tail can bend and be used as an extra paw. This means the pygmy can wind its tail around a tree branch to keep from falling to the ground.

The pygmy's favorite home is the kapok tree. The seedpods of the kapok are soft and fluffy and look much like a pygmy anteater. This natural *camouflage* helps make the pygmy invisible to its predators. A

What great camouflage: a pygmy anteater looks like a seedpod when it curls itself into a ball.

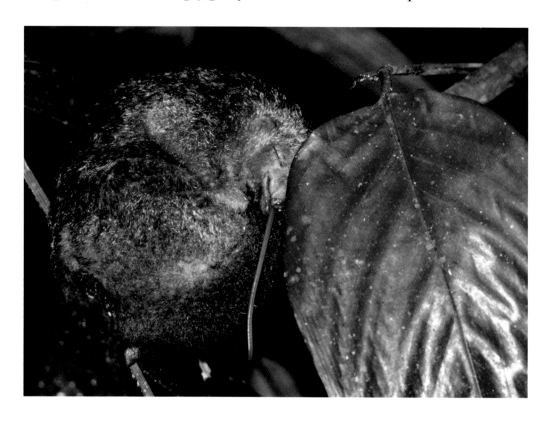

The tamandua has unusual markings. Its dark fur makes the animal appear to be wearing a vest.

hungry owl flying by might mistake the anteater for a seedpod and miss out on an easy meal. When an animal threatens or frightens a pygmy, the pygmy will emit a shrill call.

Pygmy anteaters find their meals on the leaves and branches of trees. In addition to ants and termites, pygmys enjoy eating bees, beetles, other insects, and fruit. The pygmy anteater does not have an overly long snout—in comparison to the other anteaters, it looks quite stubby. The pygmy does have a sticky

tongue and uses it to lap up ants, but when eating other foods it may use its paws to push the food into its mouth.

The tamandua anteater is a little larger than the pygmy but less than half the size of a giant anteater. It is as big as a large house cat. Its body is covered in short, thick fur. Tamanduas that live in the northern regions of South America and north into Mexico have black markings on their shoulders and body, which make the animals look as though they are wearing

16

vests. Tamanduas from the southern regions are all one color, usually tan or brown.

Tamanduas share several similarities with pygmy anteaters. They, too, have a prehensile tail. It is so strong that the tamandua can actually grasp a branch with it and hang upside down. Tamanduas are also mostly arboreal, spending their lives high in the trees of the rain forest. However, they do leave the trees on occasion and are sometimes spotted by humans.

Like other anteaters, tamanduas live by themselves. If they encounter another animal they will hiss and emit a bad-smelling, skunklike odor. Native

The tamandua has curved claws just like the giant anteater. It uses them for protection and to find food.

South Americans call this anteater the "stinker of the forest." If the horrible smell isn't enough to stop an attacker, the tamandua will stand on its hind legs and slash at an opponent with its claws. If possible, it may also wrap its long, strong arms around the other animal and squeeze tightly. A tamandua will fight to defend itself.

These medium-sized anteaters are of use to humans. Some natives will bring tamanduas into their homes to exterminate ants. Unfortunately, they are also hunted for the strong *tendons* in their tails, which are used for ropes.

Giant anteaters are quite large and appear even bigger due to their bushy tails and long tubelike snouts. From the tip of its nose to the end of its tail, a giant anteater can be up to 7 feet (2 meters) long. It lumbers along awkwardly, bearing the weight of each step on the sides of its knuckles. Its 4-inch (10 centimeters)-long claws curve inward and do not *retract*. Although this may appear to make walking difficult, the giant anteater does quite well walking or running. The animal needs those powerful claws to break through hard ground, rotting logs, and tough termite mounds, to obtain food and to defend itself from a predator. The giant anteater keeps its claws well sharpened through regular use and by scraping them on trees.

A giant anteater can smell termites from miles away. This anteater has detected a meal inside an active termite mound.

This anteater has very small ears and eyes. Giant anteaters have very poor eyesight. In fact, they can barely see beyond thirty feet. The strongest of their five senses is their sense of smell. A giant anteater literally follows its nose at dinnertime and successfully roots out deeply buried insects.

Giant anteaters are both nocturnal and *diurnal*. Anteaters that live close to humans are nocturnal. They like their privacy and prefer to search for food at night when most humans are sleeping. Diurnal anteaters generally live away from populated areas in the more remote portions of the savannas, so they are active during the day.

If a giant anteater is lucky it can live to be fourteen years old. Some anteaters raised in captivity have lived longer than twenty-five years. Many scientists study this wonderful animal to learn about its habits and survival skills. Although the giant anteater is awkwardly shaped and not usually considered beautiful, South Americans and people all over the world admire this great creature.

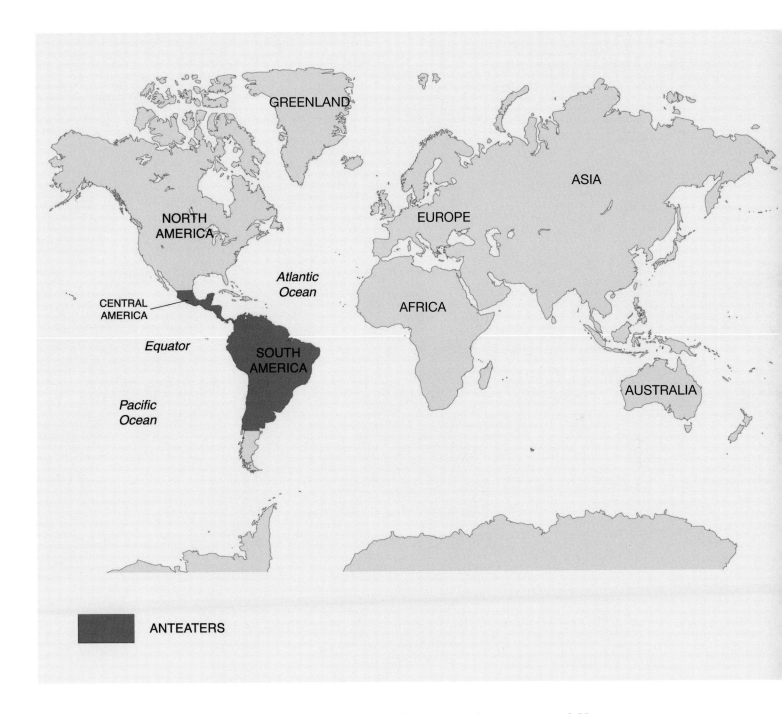

Anteaters can be found from southern Mexico to Argentina and Uruguay.

3 Growing and Learning

It is spring in the savanna. For the female giant anteater, it is time to find a mate. Like females of many other animal species, during mating season the female anteater emits a strong scent to attract a partner. Male anteaters from miles away can detect her odor. Eventually one finds his way to her territory.

He approaches her slowly and lays his head against her back to show that he is interested in her. The two anteaters playfully exchange nudges and swats; they are getting to know each other. They will spend only about one day together before mating. Then the male leaves, and the female is once again alone.

A young anteater still enjoys catching a ride on its mother's back.

After approximately six months she is ready to give birth. She stands upright, using her tail for balance. Anteaters only have one baby at a time. When the baby is born, it is already active and climbs up its mother's stiff, bristly coat to rest on her back. It burrows into her fur to keep safe and warm.

When they begin their lives, anteaters are totally dependent upon their mothers, much like human babies. Fortunately the female giant anteater is a very good parent. The mother licks her baby clean and lets it rest on her back. She will carry it around this way for many months. In this position the white stripe on the baby matches up with the white stripe on the mother. They look like one very large anteater. Once again this natural camouflage comes in handy, helping to disguise the baby and hiding it from predators. If the baby falls, it lets out a high, shrill whistle to let its mother know where to find it.

Anteaters are *mammals* and nurse their young. A baby must drink its mother's milk for several months. But while the mother digs up tasty ants for her own meal, her baby soon begins to try and catch a few ants as they scamper away. Baby anteaters learn quickly that ants and termites are tasty treats.

This mother anteater feeds on termites while her baby clings to her back. Soon enough, the baby will enjoy termites as well.

They also learn from their mothers how to protect themselves. A giant anteater mother will pretend to fight with her baby. While the baby anteater is having fun playing, it is also learning how to fight and use its claws. It stands on its hind legs and slashes

25

with its claws, copying its mother's defensive motions. When the baby plays too roughly or the mother is too tired, she will lay her head against the baby's back to calm it down.

Giant anteater babies stay close to their mothers until they are about six months old. Then they feel confident enough to venture away for short trips, but if they become frightened they rush back to the mother and climb right up on her back.

By nine months of age a young giant anteater can weigh as much as 65 pounds (29.5 kilograms). This is too much weight for the mother to continue to carry, and she begins to push her baby away. She makes the young anteater walk beside her. An anteater is full grown at two years of age. At this time mother and baby must separate. There are not enough termites and ants to feed two large anteaters in one territory. The baby begins to look for its own territory in which to live. It will never see its mother again. The young anteater will be able to have its own babies at three to four years of age, and then the cycle will continue.

A giant anteater digs at the base of a termite mound in search of a meal.

4 Big Appetites

Finding enough insects to fill a giant anteater's stomach is a full-time job. An anteater travels over its territory all day long searching out sources of food. It needs to consume about thirty thousand ants or termites a day to survive.

All of its meals are hidden deep inside nests. Ants build their nests underground. The nests are sometimes as large as football fields. Termites live inside tall mounds they build aboveground. They build these amazing structures by chewing earth and mixing it with their own *saliva*. This makes a kind of liquid cement. Termite mounds are strong and can even withstand floodwaters. Millions of termites live inside these gigantic mounds.

Termite nests can be huge and provide a home to millions of termites.

Ants and termites stay close to their nests. Each insect has a job to do and is important to the survival of the colony. Worker insects collect food from the outside and bring it back to the nest. Soldiers defend the nest. Both termites and ants have a queen. She remains deep inside the nest busily laying hundreds of eggs that will hatch into new members of the colony. The nest has many trails but is very organized. Insects scamper through the nests unaware that trouble awaits them.

A giant anteater directly above has located the nest using its powerful sense of smell. It scratches at the ground with its curved claws. One of the claws is longer than the rest. This serves as a strong tool for puncturing the hard earth. The anteater uses it to break through the ground and then pushes dirt aside with its snout to widen the hole.

The hungry anteater mounts a surprise attack. It thrusts its long, sticky, saliva-covered tongue into the nest. Ants scatter and try to outrun this dangerous intrusion. The anteater's tongue darts in and out of its mouth at a rate of more than 150 strokes per minute

Did You Know . . .

A giant anteater's sense of smell is more than forty times more powerful than a human's. It can detect food sources from miles away. This powerful sense of smell may also help the solitary animals find each other during mating season.

30

The giant anteater's snout is long and slender, perfect for sucking ants and termites from their nests.

and extends out as much as 24 inches (62 centimeters). It is covered with tiny spikes that point backward. The spikes catch the ants, which are swept inside the anteater's mouth and directly into its stomach. Along with all the ants, dirt and gravel also get sucked into the anteater's stomach.

The anteater has no teeth and can't chew its food. Instead, its stomach muscles grind up its meal. The dirt and gravel it has swallowed rolls around inside its stomach, helping to crush the ants before they are digested.

A giant anteater's tongue can be up to 24 inches (61 centimeters) long.

Anteaters consume their meals quickly. Once a nest is disturbed, soldier ants will rush to defend their home. Much like a human army, the soldier ants begin to attack. They swarm up the anteater's snout and bite its tongue. The anteater soon becomes irritated and moves on to another nest within its territory. Worker ants quickly begin to repair and rebuild the damage to their home.

While many species of ants and termites are poisonous, their bites don't hurt anteaters. An anteater eats many small meals throughout the day. It ingests tiny amounts of poison again and again. Its body becomes used to the various poisons and the animal doesn't get sick.

This natural chain of events keeps the anteater fed and makes certain its food supply remains intact. The ant and termite colonies survive the attack and will continue to flourish, at least until an anteater needs another meal.

Ants try to scatter when a giant anteater plunges its snout into their nest.

5 Endangered

Giant anteaters have few natural predators. The big cats of the savanna, such as pumas and jaguars, hunt anteaters only when they are desperate and can find no other food. They know that confronting a giant anteater can be dangerous. Anteaters are strong fighters. Their long claws can severely injure or even kill a predator. The big cats try to stay away and hunt easier *prey*.

While predators aren't a big concern, several things do endanger anteaters. For instance, natural disasters pose a threat. Floodwaters during quick, heavy downpours can sweep away anteaters, even though they can swim. The savanna also has a long,

Jaguars are predators that have been known to hunt anteaters in the wild.

hot dry season when many fires break out. Anteaters, with their long, coarse hair, catch fire easily and perish. However, their main source of danger is from the human species. Anteaters are *endangered* because humans are destroying their *habitats.*

What is happening in the Cerrado, the largest savanna region in South America, is a good example of the devastation that is occurring. Farmers are clearing much of the land of the Cerrado to plant crops. Tractors cut into the brush and tall grass, tearing it out of the earth. When the natural vegetation is cleared, soybeans and other cash crops are planted. The soybean crop earns money the farmers need to feed their families, but farming destroys the habitat of many important animals, insects, and plants.

Land is being cleared in many areas where anteaters live, causing them to lose their natural habitats.

More than 160 types of mammals, 800 birds, and more than 100 reptile species live in the Cerrado. It is also home to more than 10,000 different types of plants. Almost all of the Cerrado, like many other savannas, has been disturbed by humans. Farming is only one problem. Humans are also developing some of the land for housing. Only a little more than 1 percent of the Cerrado has been declared a protected area.

As the land is developed for housing and crops, the giant anteaters' food source is destroyed. Ant nests and termite mounds disappear. With less food available, fewer and fewer anteaters can survive.

The pygmy and tamandua anteaters face a similar fate in the rain forest. The destruction of their home by humans is a far greater danger than the one they face from their natural predators: eagles, owls, and hawks. The great rain forests are being plundered. For many years native groups harvested sap from the rubber trees doing little harm, but now other resources are being taken. Large companies drill for oil that lies deep beneath the forest. Chemical companies harvest plants to make medicine. But by far the most severe threat to the rain forest is from *logging*.

Many people throughout the world want the exotic wood that grows in the rain forest. It is used for furniture and decorative items, and in homes. Tropical timber is highly valued and brings a good profit for

Many farmers in the rain forests use the slash-and-burn method to clear the land.

the businesses that harvest it. Laws made to protect the rain forest are not always enforced. Most of the logging is done illegally, yet it continues unabated.

Farmers in the rain forest also clear the trees to plant crops using the slash-and-burn method. First, they cut away the small shrubs and trees. Then they chop down the larger trees that form the forest canopy. This canopy is the home of the tamandua and pygmy anteater and many other animals. The trees are left on the ground. The dying trees release nutrients that enrich the earth. When the trees are dry, the farmers burn them and then plant their crops. The slash-and-burn method creates rich soil that helps the crops, but it destroys acres of forest.

If the trees were replanted it would take decades, or longer, for them to grow to maturity. In most cases there are no plans to replant them at all. Rain forests used to cover about 14 percent of the world. Now they cover less than 6 percent. The rain forest is being destroyed at a staggering rate of 150 acres per minute around the world.

Did You Know . . .

Tamanduas are the most common anteaters on Earth. They are even being bred in captivity in some zoos. This is quite difficult due to their specialized diet of termites, bees, and honey. Giant anteaters in captivity eat a special gruel consisting of birds-of-prey meat, fruit, yogurt, and cricket legs. But zookeepers know the hard work of caring for anteaters is worth it.

Conservation groups are actively fighting to save the rain forests and savannas. They are trying to get stricter laws passed that will keep the land in its natural state. They also serve as watchdogs, trying to make certain the laws that are in place are enforced. Hopefully, conservation groups can exert enough pressure to stop the destruction before it is too late.

Many other conservation groups are specifically focused on protecting wildlife. They keep a diligent watch on different species and track their numbers. These groups try to find out which animals are dying out. They track their breeding, the number of young being born, how long the animals are living, and where they are living. They publish lists that tell which animals are in trouble. Anteaters are listed as "vulnerable" and "threatened" by some groups.

Like these gentle creatures, many wonderful varieties of animal and plant life are disappearing and endangered because humans are invading and destroying their habitats. Anteaters' natural homes must be protected or the world will lose anteaters forever.

If their habitats are protected, anteaters will be around for many more generations.

Glossary

arboreal: Existing in trees.

camouflage: Having an appearance that makes something blend in with its surroundings.

diurnal: To be active during the day.

endangered: Threatened with becoming extinct.

extinct: To no longer exist.

girdle: Something that encircles or confines.

habitat: The place where an animal lives.

logging: The process of removing timber from a forest.

mammals: Animals that have hair, give birth to live young, and nurse them with their own milk.

nocturnal: To be active at night.

pelvic: The bones of the hips located below the spine.

predator: An animal that hunts another animal.

prehensile: Adapted for grasping by wrapping around an object.

prey: An animal that is hunted by another animal.

retract: To draw back.

saliva: Liquid secreted into the mouth that helps digestion.

savanna: Grassland containing scattered trees.

tendon: Tough cord of fibrous tissue that connects muscle to bone or other parts.

territorial: An instinct to protect and defend the area in which one lives.

vertebrae: Bones that make up the backbone.

Find Out More

Books

Dollar, Sam. *Anteaters*. Austin, TX: Raintree Steck-Vaughn, 2001.

Kite, Lorien. *Nature's Children: Anteaters*. Danbury, CT: Grolier Educational, 1999.

Lee, Sandra. *Anteaters*. Chanhassen, MN: The Child's World, Inc., 1999.

Squire, Ann O. *Anteaters, Sloths, and Armadillos*. New York: Franklin Watts, 1999.

Web Sites

The Chaffee Zoo
www.chaffeezoo.org/animals/anteaters.html

The Online Anteater
www.maiaw.com/anteater

The San Francisco Zoo
www.sfzoo.org/cgi-bin/animals.py?ID=29

Index

Page numbers for illustrations are in **boldface**.

About the Author

Renee C. Rebman has published several nonfiction books for young readers. She is also a published playwright. Her plays have been produced in schools and community theaters across the country.